O. HENRY'S
The Gift of the Magi

adaptation, music, and lyrics by
Peter Ekstrom

"Acting Edition prepared by Jim Kramer"

SAMUEL FRENCH, INC.
45 WEST 25TH STREET   NEW YORK 10010
7623 SUNSET BOULEVARD   HOLLYWOOD 90046
LONDON   TORONTO

Copyright ©, 1981, 1984, by Peter Ekstrom

ALL RIGHTS RESERVED

Amateurs wishing to arrange for the production of THE GIFT OF THE MAGI must make application to SAMUEL FRENCH, INC., at 45 West 25th Street, New York, N.Y. 10010, giving the following particulars:

(1) The name of the town and theatre or hall in which the production is to take place.
(2) The maximum seating capacity of the theatre or hall.
(3) Scale of ticket prices.
(4) The number of performances it is intended to give, and the dates thereof.

Upon receipt of these particulars SAMUEL FRENCH, INC., will quote terms and availability.

Stock royalty quoted on application to SAMUEL FRENCH, INC., 45 West 25th Street, New York, N.Y. 10010.

For all other rights than those stipulated above, apply to Writers & Artists Agency, 162 West 56th Street, New York, N.Y. 10019.

A Piano conductor score will be loaned two months prior to the production ONLY on receipt of the royalty quoted for all performances, the rental fee and a refundable deposit. The deposit will be refunded on the safe return to SAMUEL FRENCH, INC. of the material loaned for the production.

No part of this book may be reproduced, stored in a retrieval system, or transmitted in any form, by any means, including mechanical, electronic, photocopying, recording, or otherwise, without the prior written permission of the publisher.

Anyone presenting the play shall not commit or authorize any act or omission by which the copyright of the play or the right to copyright same may be impaired.

No changes shall be made in the play for the purpose of your production unless authorized in writing.

The publication of this play does not imply that it is necessarily available for performance by amateurs or professionals. Amateurs and professionals considering a production are strongly advised in their own interests to apply to Samuel French, Inc., for consent before starting rehearsals, advertising, or booking a theatre or hall.

Printed in U.S.A.

ISBN 0 573 68132 5

Actors Theatre of Louisville
The State Theatre of Kentucky
Jon Jory, *Producing-Director*

Presents

December 1 through the 26, 1981

O. HENRY'S

The Gift of the Magi

adaptation, music, and lyrics by

Peter Ekstrom

Directed by Larry Deckel

Musical Direction	Peter Ekstrom
Set Design	Paul Owen
Costume Design	Jess Goldstein
Lighting Design	Karl Haas
Co-Property Masters	Sam Garst
	Sandra Strawn
Stage Managers	Benita Hofstetter
	Craig Weindling

Cast of Characters

Della .... BEVERLY LAMBERT
Jim .... PETER BOYNTON

It is the Christmas Eve of 1905 in New York City.

Additional lyrics for "Tomorrow is Christmas" by Ted Enik.

Copyright © of THE GIFT OF THE MAGI
1981 Lyrics and Music by Peter Ekstrom

This work is dedicated to Elizabeth Kelly.

CHARACTERS

DELLA — a young woman
JIM — her husband

TIME — 1905, the morning of Christmas Eve and that night

PLACE — Their one-room flat in New York City. They are very poor; the furniture is shabby. There is a bed with a chest at its foot, a dresser, a dressing table with a mirror (but for a theatrical effect there is no glass in the mirror), a kitchen table with two chairs, a small stove and sink, a small rocker and an armoire. There are two windows. Perhaps one looks out on to a brick wall, the other to the street if you were to look down. It is snowing.

NOTE: Care should be taken that this show be directed and acted as simply and honestly as possible.

The Gift of the Magi

Scene 1

MUSIC CUE #1 – "Mini Overture" segue to MUSIC CUE #2 – "Opening Song" Lights come up. It is the morning of Christmas Eve. DELLA, in camisole and bloomers, is at her dressing table pinning up the last of her hair. JIM is in bed under the blankets and sings his part in the following song completely covered by them. There is some movement on his part, but his face and body don't emerge until the end.

Della. (*singing*)
JIM, JIM, JIM DARLING
WAKE UP AND FACE THE DAY
(*There is no response from JIM. DELLA crosses to bed.*)
JIM, JIM, JIM DARLING
  Jim. (*singing*)
LEAVE ME ALONE! GO AWAY! GO AWAY!
  Della.
FACE THE DAY!
  Jim.
GO AWAY!
  Della.
FACE THE DAY!
  Jim.
GO AWAY!

(*During this next lyric, DELLA crosses to dressing table, gets empty pitcher and goes to the sink.*)

Della.
JIM, IT'S TIME TO GET UP.
  Jim. (*almost a yawn but still singing*)
AH, AH, AH . . .
  Della.
TIME TO OPEN YOUR EYES.
  Jim.
AH, AH, AH
  Della.   Jim.
TIME TO LIFT YOURSELF   AH, IT'S COLD

THE GIFT OF THE MAGI

UP OUT OF SLUMBER-
   LAND.
JIM, IT'S TIME TO ARISE!
AND I WANT TO
   SLEEP
A LITTLE MORE.

(*DELLA pretends to fill pitcher with water in case JIM sees.*)

DELLA.
JIM, IT'S TIME TO GET UP.
   JIM.
AH, AH, AH . . .
   DELLA.
TIME TO GET OUT OF BED.
   JIM.
AH, AH, AH

DELLA.
IF YOU DON'T
I WILL TAKE THIS
   COLD WATER
AND DUMP IT OVER
   YOUR HEAD!
   JIM.
YOU WOULDN'T DARE.
   DELLA. (*She tiptoes to bed in time with music.*)
YES I WOULD!
   JIM. (*pokes his head out and sees the pitcher*)
YOU WOULDN'T DARE.
   DELLA.
YES I WOULD!

JIM.
AH, IT'S COLD
AND I WANT TO SLEEP

A LITTLE MORE.

(*On this last "WOULD", DELLA lunges toward JIM. He leaps out of bed just in time. He is wearing faded and patched red long-johns as he says:*)

   JIM. Wait! Della, stop!
   DELLA. (*showing him the pitcher is empty*) Only fooling!
   JIM. Ahh! I'll get you later!
   DELLA. If you can!

(*MUSIC CUE: #3 – "Tomorrow is Christmas".* During this

---

*Additional lyrics by Ted Enik

song DELLA is quite happy. JIM is a little sad, but not so sad that he doesn't smile now and then. This song is not a dance, but each should feel the music with their actions as they go about their morning rituals. Suggested activities: JIM stretches. JIM pulls his pants out from under the mattress. DELLA fills pitcher with warm water and pours it into JIM's washing bowl. JIM opens shutters. DELLA puts petticoat over bloomers. DELLA gets JIM's shirt from the back of a chair. She helps JIM with shirt, fastens cufflinks, etc.)

BOTH. (*They give each other a quick morning kiss on the first note of the song.*)
TOMORROW IS CHRISTMAS, THE TIME TO BE MERRY
WITH WREATHES TIED WITH RIBBONS AS RED AS A
  BERRY
THE CANDLES AND HOLLY CHASE WORRIES AWAY
FOR TOMORROW IS CHRISTMAS DAY . . .

TOMORROW IS CHRISTMAS WHEN SPIRITS ARE
  LIGHTER
THE SPARKLE OF SNOW MAKES THE CITY SEEM
  BRIGHTER
AND EVERYTHING LOOKS LIKE A WINDOW DISPLAY
FOR TOMORROW IS CHRISTMAS DAY . . .

LOOK OUTSIDE AND A STAR ABOVE
WILL SHINE AS A GUIDE TO US ALL
JOY WILL COME WHEN WE GIVE OUR LOVE
NO MATTER HOW GREAT OR HOW SMALL

A SMILE IN THE MORNING, A CHILD IN A MANGER
A GIFT FROM THE HEART TO A FRIEND OR A
  STRANGER
THE WARMTH OF A WORLD GETTING READY TO SAY
THAT TOMORROW IS CHRISTMAS, CHRISTMAS
  DAY . . .
TOMORROW IS CHRISTMAS DAY. . . .

(*At the end of the song JIM sits. DELLA goes to stove.*)

DELLA. Would you like a muffin, Jim? (*JIM rises and moves to dressing table.*)

JIM. I'm not hungry this morning, Dell, (*JIM sits at dressing table. There is a pause. DELLA is curious about JIM's response to her question. She hums or la-dee-dah's the tune to "Tomorrow is Christmas" as she pours two cups of coffee.*)
DELLA. Some coffee? (*There is no response from JIM. Instead he is lathering soap and preparing to shave.*) Jim?
JIM. What?
DELLA. Coffee?
JIM. (*starting to shave*) Oh . . . yes, of course . . . coffee.

(*DELLA continues her humming as she crosses to the window, opens it, shivers and brings bottle of milk in from ledge. DELLA crosses back and pours milk into coffee.*)

DELLA. (*bringing coffee to him*) Darling, what is it? Didn't you sleep well? (*no response*) Jim!?
JIM. (*shaving throughout*) I love you, Dell.
DELLA. Of course you do! I love you too.
JIM. But what kind of a husband am I?
DELLA. (*crossing to bed to get her shoes*) Why, you're the best husband in the world!

(*During the next speech DELLA sits on bed and fastens one of her shoes.*)

JIM. Oh Della! Would the best husband in the world have his wife live in a fifth floor walk-up with only cold water complete with stained and torn furniture? Would he leave her there alone all day while he works at his job as a clerk in "NEW YORK CITY" that brought a meager twenty dollars a week which could barely pay the rent and the bills, let alone leave enough to buy food to keep her alive?
DELLA. Jim—
JIM. (*He turns and looks at her.*) Would the best husband in the world wake up to such a beautiful face on the morning of Christmas Eve knowing that he couldn't save, borrow or beg enough money to buy his wife a Christmas present? (*JIM nicks his lip. He is done shaving and begins to wash his face.*)
DELLA. (*crossing to him, one shoe on*) So that's it! . . . Jim, listen to me. When I married you and took your name, Mrs. James Dillingham Young (!) I knew things were going to be difficult for a while. But I loved you. And I love you now . . . and

tomorrow I'll feel just the same. (*She wipes excess soap off JIM's face.*) If it will make you feel any better, I can tell you that I don't have a Christmas present for you either! Now have a muffin, boy! See, we're not starving! . . . Come on, smile! (*DELLA sings to cheer him up.*)
'TIS THE SEASON TO BE JOLLY
FA LA LA LA LA . . LA LA LA
LAAAAAAAAAAAAAAAAAEEEEEEEEEEEEEEEH!

(*The last "LA" is rather a shriek, for when she hits it. JIM has jumped up and began to tickle her wildly. DELLA is the sort so ticklish that just to look at her tickle spots makes her burst into uncontrollable laughter. MUSIC CUE #4 — "Now I've Got You!" comes on this last "LA." Movement in this song should be fun, but not so wild that it interferes with very difficult singing. If this song proves too difficult for the players, a short tickle/chase scene may be substituted using lyrics from the song as spoken dialogue while JIM chases DELLA around their apartment.*)

JIM. (*sings*)
NOW I'VE GOT YOU!
DELLA.
STOP IT! YAH HA HA HA HA HA
JIM.
NOW I'VE GOT YOU!
DELLA.
STOP IT! YAH HA HA HA HA HA
JIM.
NOW I'VE GOT YOU!
DELLA.
STOP IT YAH HA HA HA HA HA
BOTH.
HA HA HA HA HA HA HA HA HA HA HA
JIM.
WHAT'S THE MATTER?
DELLA.
STOP IT! YAH HA HA HA HA HA
JIM.
WHAT'S THE MATTER?
DELLA.
STOP IT! YAH HA HA HA HA HA

JIM.
WHAT'S THE MATTER?
DELLA.
STOP IT! YAH HA HA HA HA
BOTH.
HA HA HA HA HA HA HA!

JIM.	DELLA.
ALL I WANT TO DO MY DEAR	JIM! AH! NO! AH!
IS TOUCH YOU THERE AND TOUCH YOU HERE!	PLEASE, AH! STOP IT!
DON'T BE TIMID, DON'T BE FRIGHTENED	JIM JIM, NO NO!
DON'T YOU WANT TO HUG ME, DARLING?	PLEASE STOP! AAAHH!

JIM.
NOW I'VE GOT YOU!
DELLA.
STOP IT! YAH HA HA HA HA HA
JIM.
NOW I'VE GOT YOU!
DELLA.
STOP IT! YAH HA HA HA HA HA
JIM.
NOW I'VE GOT YOU!
DELLA.
STOP IT! YAH HA HA HA HA HA
BOTH.
HA HA HA HA HA HA HA HA HA HA HA
HA HA HA HA HA HA HA HA HA HA HA . . . ETC.

(*They end up on the bed, laughing in a loving embrace.*)

JIM. Oh . . . my Della . . . you are so beautiful!
DELLA. (*blushing*) Jim!
JIM. Tomorrow is Christmas . . . will you wear your hair down for me? (*There is a pause. JIM tickles DELLA again.*)
DELLA. Anything!

(*During the next speech DELLA puts her other shoe on.*)

JIM. I love it when you wear your hair down. You have the

THE GIFT OF THE MAGI

most beautiful hair in the world! (*with light-hearted pomp*) Why if the Queen of Sheeba lived in the flat across the airshaft, you would have to let your hair hang out the window someday to dry, just to depreciate Her Majesty's jewels and gifts!

DELLA. (*laughing*) Oh Jim! (*DELLA goes to chest to get her blouse. JIM to armoire to get his vest.*)
JIM. Della . . . I want so much for you . . . you know that?
DELLA. It will come with time, Jim.
JIM. Will it?

(*MUSIC CUE #4a — "Intro to If We Had Money".*)

JIM. (*continued*) I'm just so tired of being poor.
DELLA. It will come with time.
JIM. Yes, but — If we had money . . .

(*MUSIC CUE #5 — "If We Had Money". During the first lyrics of this song, DELLA puts her skirt on, and JIM helps her fasten it.*)

JIM. (*sings*)
IF WE HAD MONEY I'D BUY YOU A GOWN
MADE ALL OF VELVET AND LACE!
WE'D HIRE A CARRIAGE AND TROT THROUGH THE TOWN
AT A LEISURELY PACE . . .
DELLA.
WE'D STOP AT A RESTAURANT AND ORDER A MEAL
ASPARAGUS TIPS AND A BLANQUETTE OF VEAL
AND WE'D TOAST TO THE WONDERFUL WAY
   THAT WE'D FEEL . . .
JIM.
IF WE HAD MONEY.
BOTH.
IF WE HAD MONEY.

(*JIM gets his shoes and sits to put them on.*)

DELLA.
IF WE HAD MONEY I'D BUY YOU SOME SHOES
OF LEATHER IMPORTED FROM SPAIN!
WE'D TRIP DOWN THE AVENUE TAPPING OUR HEELS
TO A JOYOUS REFRAIN . . .

JIM.
WE'D STOP IN A BALLROOM WITH LIGHTS ALL
  A-GLOW
AND REQUEST THAT THEY PLAY EVERY WALTZ
  THAT THEY KNOW
AND WE'D SMILE ALL THE WHILE AS WE DANCED
  TO-AND-FRO
  DELLA.
IF WE HAD MONEY.
  BOTH.
IF WE HAD MONEY.
  DELLA.
ALL I REALLY NEED, JIM
IS YOU CLOSE BY MY SIDE
  JIM.
IF WE HAD MONEY I'D RENT YOU A FLAT
THAT HAD CUSHIONS OF SILK IN THE CHAIRS WHERE
  WE SAT
AND BRIGHT REGAL BANNERS WOULD ALL BE
  UNFURLED
FOR IF WE HAD MONEY I'D BUY YOU THE WORLD!

DELLA.	JIM.
IF WE HAD MONEY	IF WE HAD MONEY
WE'D WORRY AND FRET	ALL CARES WOULD RETREAT
TRYING TO KEEP THIEVES AWAY	FOREVER SECURE WE WOULD STAY
INSTEAD OF THE BURDEN	INSTEAD OF THE BURDEN
OF BEING IN DEBT	OF MAKING ENDS MEET
WE'D HAVE TAXES TO PAY!	WE COULD GIVE HALF OUR RICHES AWAY!
JIM. (*picking up a stack of bills*)	DELLA.
THE COOKING AND WASH	
WOULD BE DONE BY A MAID	JIM, I DON'T MIND.
WE'D AWAKE EVERY MORNING	
AND BE UNDISMAYED	I'M HAPPY NOW!

FOR AT LAST ALL OUR
  BILLS
WOULD BE FINALLY
  PAID!
(*He throws bills in the air.*)
  DELLA.
IF WE HAD MONEY.
  BOTH.
IF WE HAD MONEY.

JIM.	DELLA.
ALL THE THINGS I WANT, DELL	ALL I REALLY NEED, JIM
TO KEEP YOU SATISFIED!	IS YOU CLOSE BY MY SIDE . . .

  DELLA.
IT DOESN'T MATTER, I'D STILL BE IN BLISS
IF YOU GAVE ME THE WORLD OR JUST GAVE ME A
  KISS
AND BECAUSE WE ARE POOR THERE'S NO REASON
  FOR SHAME
FOR IF WE HAD MONEY . . .
  JIM.
IF WE HAD MONEY . . .
  DELLA.
IF WE HAD MONEY . . .
I'D LOVE YOU THE SAME!
  BOTH.
IF WE HAD MONEY I'D LOVE YOU
LOVE YOU THE SAME!
(*They end the song in an embrace.*)

DELLA. What time is it, Jim? You don't want to be late for work.

JIM. I wish I could spend all day right here with my girl. But I suppose it is time for me to go.

DELLA. (*moving to stove*) Well take out your watch, darling, and see.

(*JIM turns his back to her and to the audience so no one can see the watch as he looks at the time and puts the watch back in his pocket.*)

JIM. It's seven-fifteen.

THE GIFT OF THE MAGI

DELLA. Oh, good! (*a pause*) Let me look at your watch, Jim.
JIM. (*putting bow tie and armbands on*) Why?
DELLA. Because it's so pretty. We may not have money, but that watch is certainly a treasure for you. I remember when your mother gave it to you, after your father passed on. Let's have a look at it. (*JIM does nothing.*) Why are you always so embarrassed to take it out? It really is a treasure.
JIM. You know why . . .
DELLA. Because your mother lost the chain and you carry the watch on a leather strap? Jim! (*She laughs.*) Don't be a silly-willy! Come on!

(*MUSIC CUE #5a—"Watch Music." JIM starts to take watch out, and DELLA helps him. He holds it up in the air by the leather strap. There is a change of light, and the watch seems to glow!*)

DELLA. (*continued*) Oooooo! It's really quite a beauty, Jim. (*with light-hearted pomp*) You know, if King Solomon were our janitor, with all his treasures piled up in the basement, you could pull out your watch every time you passed, just to see him pluck at his beard from envy! (*They both laugh.*)

(*MUSIC CUE #6—"Look at my Watch". The lights change. The room lights dim. The special stays on watch. Special up on JIM's face. This song is JIM's internal sentiment. While he is singing DELLA straightens up the apartment, makes the bed and doesn't notice JIM. Again, for DELLA this is not choreographed, but she should feel the music and tone in her movements. JIM remains stationary throughout.*)

JIM. (*sings*)
LOOK AT MY WATCH
SEE HOW IT SHINES
IT ONCE BELONGED TO MY FATHER
IT'S MADE OF GOLD, WITH A FINE CHINA FACE
AND THE CRYSTAL HAS NO SCRATCH UPON IT . . .

SEE HOW THE HANDS
MOVE PAST THE NUMBERS
MARKING THE MINUTES AND HOURS
WITH STEADY PULSE THEY COUNT THE TIME

THE GIFT OF THE MAGI

IF I WIND IT UP ONCE IN THE MORNING . . .
(*He sings to DELLA but she does not yet notice him.*)
MY LOVE FOR YOU SHINES JUST AS BRIGHT
IT'S PURE AS ANY GOLD COULD BE
WITH STEADY PULSE MY HEART COUNTS TIME
I DON'T HAVE TO WIND IT
IT NEVER RUNS DOWN . . .

(*DELLA sits at dressing table and applies finishing touches with powder puff in mirror.*)

I TOUCH YOUR SOFT HANDS
I LOOK AT YOUR FACE
I STARE IN YOUR EYES AND SEE
THAT YOU ARE MY ONLY REAL TREASURE
YOU ARE MY ONLY REAL TREASURE . . .

(*Now DELLA sees JIM's reflection in the mirror. She turns to him, and as she turns JIM looks back at his watch.*)

LOOK AT MY WATCH
SEE HOW IT SHINES
IT ONCE BELONGED TO MY FATHER
IT'S MADE OF GOLD, WITH A FINE CHINA FACE
(*Now JIM and DELLA face each other.*)
BUT YOU ARE MY ONLY REAL TREASURE . . .
(*Lights back to normal.*)

JIM. And now—(*He closes the watch with a snap.*) It really is time for me to go to work. (*JIM goes to armoire to get his jacket. DELLA goes to coat tree to get his overcoat.*)

DELLA. Don't forget your coat, Jim. It's cold out there. (*helping him into overcoat*) Maybe today they'll give you a promotion. Maybe today they'll make you President of the Company!

JIM. (*laughing*) I love you Dell.

(*JIM gives DELLA a quick goodbye kiss. MUSIC CUE #6a— "Money Underscoring". DELLA puts JIM's hat on for him. JIM exits.*)

DELLA. (*at door, calling to him*) Don't work too hard. Tomorrow is Christmas, and you won't have to work at all! (*DELLA makes sure he's gone, then she runs to her secret hiding place and produces a can filled with pennies and proudly holds it up.*) Oh, Della! You are so sly. All this talk of being poor, when here lies a fortune . . . (*She shakes the can, and the pennies rattle.*) in pennies . . . but a fortune none the less! (*DELLA crosses to the table and sits. She opens can and takes out a handkerchief and places it flat on the table. She dumps out all the coins on this handkerchief and begins counting them in tens over a musical vamp.*) Ten . . . twenty . . . thirty . . . Jim is going to be so surprised! . . . fifty . . . sixty . . . seventy . . . eighty . . . He doesn't know it but . . . ninety . . . for five months I've scrimped at the butchers, with the vegetable man . . . one dollar! . . . everywhere . . . because this Christmas, more than anything . . . twenty . . . thirty . . . I want to be able to buy Jim a gift — (*She pauses from her counting and the vamp stops momentarily.*) a beautiful gift . . . a gift worthy of the honor of being his. (*Vamp starts again.*) sixty . . . seventy . . . eighty . . . one . . . two . . . three . . . four . . . five . . . six . . . seven! (*She stands.*) One dollar and eighty-seven cents! (*She suddenly realizes it's hardly anything and makes a face.*) One dollar and eighty-seven cents. . . ? (*DELLA sits down again.*)

(*MUSIC CUE #7 — "What Can I Give Him?"*)

DELLA. (*singing*)
I'VE SAVED THESE PENNIES FOR MONTHS UPON
  MONTHS
JUST TO FIND THAT THE SUM IS TOO SMALL . . .
I'VE TRIED MY HARDEST, BUT ONE-EIGHTY-SEVEN
WILL BUY NEXT TO NOTHING AT ALL
(*She rises.*)
DOWN IN THE STREET I SEE PEOPLE WITH PACKAGES
TIED UP IN SATIN BOWS
TREASURES THEY PURCHASED IN CHRISTMAS SHOP
  WINDOWS
AND NOW TAKEN HOME TO THOSE
THEY LOVE, TO THOSE THEY CHERISH
THEIR HUSBANDS, THEIR CHILDREN, THEIR
  FRIENDS . . .
(*She slowly walks around as she sings, stopping now and then.*)
BUT WHAT CAN I GIVE HIM?
WHAT CAN I OFFER?
WHAT CAN I GIVE HIM?
WHAT CAN THESE PENNIES BUY?

THE GIFT OF THE MAGI

HOW CAN HE KNOW MY LOVE IS GOOD AS GOLD?
I WANT TO SHOW MY LOVE WITH SOMETHING HE
  CAN HAVE AND HE CAN HOLD

BUT WHAT CAN I GIVE HIM?
WHAT CAN I OFFER?
WHAT CAN I GIVE HIM?
WHAT CAN THESE PENNIES BUY?

WITHOUT A GIFT FOR HIM
MY HEART WILL SURELY DIE . . .

WHY ARE THESE PENNIES SO FEW?
(*She wraps them up in handkerchief.*)
THIS IS THE BEST I COULD DO . . .
(*She picks it up and carries it with her.*)
DOWN ON THE SIDEWALK I HEAR CHRISTMAS
  CAROLERS
SINGING A JOYOUS SONG
STANZAS THAT SPEAK OF THE SPIRIT OF GIVING
AND TELL US: IT WON'T BE LONG
BEFORE WE START THE HOLIDAY!
SOON WE WILL CELEBRATE!
CHRISTMAS IS HERE!

WHAT CAN I GIVE HIM?
WHAT CAN I OFFER?
WHAT CAN THESE PENNIES BUY?

AND I ONLY WANTED CHRISTMAS DAY
TO BE SUCH A HAPPY HOLIDAY
I DID MY BEST, I GAVE MY HARDEST TRY
BUT WITHOUT A GIFT FOR HIM
MY HEART WILL SURELY DIE
MY HEART WILL SURELY DIE . . .
(*DELLA ends the song at the bed. Sits with the music. And she is crying a little bit.*)

(*MUSIC CUE #7a—"What Can I Give Him—Underscore."*
  DELLA rises and talks to herself.)

  DELLA. Well, Mrs. James Dillingham Young . . . you did what you could . . . Tomorrow is Christmas . . . and you have no present for Jim. You might as well not cry over something you can't do anything about. (*She sees herself in the mirror.*) Look how red and puffy your eyes are! If someone saw you right now they would think you had just found your little pet kitten frozen dead in the snow . . . (*This thought snaps her out of trance.*) My goodness! What a horrible thought! (*She puts bundle of pennies back in can.*) Tomorrow is Christmas . . . and tomorrow Jim will be home ALL day . . . and tomorrow I shall let my hair down . . . like this! (*She loosens her pins and her beautiful hair cascades to below her knees! There is a change of light, and her hair seems to glow! She picks up her brush and slowly combs.*) I really do love my hair . . . my mother once said it was too pretty to ever cut . . . and so I never have . . . I imagine someday it will grow so long that it could stretch all the way to . . . Brooklyn! (*She slowly rotates, playing with her hair.*) Jim loves it when my hair is down . . . He says I look as pretty and as graceful as a weeping willow . . . (*She smiles.*) I really do love my hair . . . (*Suddenly, an idea comes to her and flashes in her eyes.*) Wait a minute! (*Music stops.*) My HAIR!! (*Music starts again. Lights back to normal. DELLA runs about opening up drawers and furiously pulling things out in a mad search.*) Where did I put that card? . . . It must be here somewhere . . . Ah ha! Here it is!

(*She holds up an advertisement card and reads (sings) it off. MUSIC CUE #8 — "Madam Sofronie."*)

DELLA. (*singing*)
MADAM SOFRONIE, HAIR GOODS OF ALL KINDS
NEED A WIG? NEED A FALL?
DO NOT HESITATE TO CALL!
(*She speaks over music.*) Madam Sofronie's! It's on Fourteenth Street. I remember the hair-pieces in the window.
(*singing*)
IF YOU WANT THE MEN TO SMILE
WE HAVE JUST THE LATEST STYLE
GUARANTEED TO MAKE THE FELLOWS ROLL THEIR
    EYES
FOR A LITTLE BIT OF FUN
TRY A BRAID OR TRY A BUN
WE HAVE EVERYTHING IN EVERY SHAPE AND
    SIZE . . .
(*In small print at the bottom she sings:*)

BY THE WAY . . .
ALL OF OUR GOODS ARE MADE FROM GENUINE
  HUMAN HAIR
IF YOU NEED EXTRA CASH THEN STOP IN
AND MADAM SOFRONIE WILL PAY YOU
ACCORDING TO ITS BEAUTY
A VERY GOOD PRICE FOR YOUR HAIR.

(*MUSIC CUE #8a—"Melodrama".*)

DELLA. I knew I wasn't dreaming! There it is in print: "will pay you a very good price for your hair" . . . a very good price . . . Why, I'm sure I could get a small fortune for mine! And that, plus my pennies would certainly be enough to buy a nice gift for Jim! (*Music stops. She considers.*) I'll do it!!!

(*MUSIC CUE #8b—"End Scene 1." DELLA throws her hair back, grabs the can of pennies, begins to put her shawl on, hesitates for a second, then finally makes up her mind and exits so that the door slams on the final beat of the music.*)

Scene 2

Segue to MUSIC CUE #9—"Entre Scene". During this music DELLA changes wigs offstage. Segue to MUSIC CUE #10—"Opening Scene 2". It is evening now, and the stage is dimly lit. The stars have come out, and the fireplace glows. DELLA enters with her shawl covering her hair. She is carrying a small wrapped package. She looks at it and smiles, then crosses and places it on the mantle. She turns the switch which lights the gas lamps, and the stage lights come up to normal. She goes to dressing table and stands in front of the mirror. She drops her shawl revealing her now short hair to the audience. The music pauses.

DELLA. Oh, my! (*Music again as DELLA grabs her brush and furiously pulls it through her hair trying to repair the damage. The music pauses.*) If Jim doesn't kill me before he takes a second look at me, he'll say I look like a Coney Island Chorus Girl. (*Music again.*) But what could I do—oh, what could I do with a dollar and eighty-seven cents? (*The music changes as DELLA says a little prayer.*) Please God, please make him think I am still pretty. (*The slamming of a door is heard and JIM coming up the stairs la-dee-dahing the tune of "Tomorrow is Christmas." DELLA runs about as she says:*) He's home! Oh! Oh! Should I hide?

(*JIM's la-dee-dahing stops, and the music changes as DELLA makes one final touch in the mirror and positions herself for JIM's entrance. Music stops, door opens, and JIM enters carrying a wrapped present.*)

DELLA. (*aside*) Maybe he won't notice!
JIM. (*dumbfounded and dead-pan and standing still*) Dell. Your hair is gone.

(*MUSIC CUE #11 — "Your Hair is Gone!" During this song it is absolutely essential that JIM remains totally dead-pan.*)

JIM. (*singing*)
YOUR HAIR IS GONE
DELLA.
PLEASE DON'T BE MAD!
JIM.
YOUR HAIR IS GONE
DELLA.
DOES IT LOOK BAD?

JIM.	DELLA.
YOURHAIRISGONEYOUR HAIRISGONE	LET ME EXPLAIN, JIM
YOURHAIRISGONEYOUR HAIRISGONE	LET ME EXPLAIN
YOURHAIRISGONEYOUR HAIRISGONE	LET ME EXPLAIN, JIM
YOURHAIRISGONEYOUR HAIRISGONE	LET ME EXPLAIN

(*JIM turns to leave, still holding his present, then turns around and enters again.*)

JIM.
YOUR HAIR IS GONE

THE GIFT OF THE MAGI

DELLA.
YES EVERY TRESS!
JIM.
YOUR HAIR IS GONE
DELLA.
IS IT A MESS?

(*During this next lyric JIM places his wrapped present on the dressing table and crosses the room. DELLA follows. Then JIM turns around and focuses on her hair as DELLA backs away.*)

JIM.	DELLA.
YOURHAIRISGONEYOURHAIRISGONE	LET ME EXPLAIN, JIM
YOURHAIRISGONEYOURHAIRISGONE	LET ME EXPLAIN
YOURHAIRISGONEYOURHAIRISGONE	LET ME EXPLAIN, JIM
YOURHAIRISGONEYOURHAIRISGONE	LET ME EXPLAIN
DELLA. (*aside*)	JIM. (*to himself*)
COULD IT BE HE'S LOST HIS MIND?	YOUR HAIR IS GONE
HE KEEPS REPEATING WHAT HE SAYS	YOUR HAIR IS GONE
IS HE TEASING? IS HE SCOLDING?	YOUR HAIR IS GONE
IS HE GOING TO KILL ME ON THE SPOT?	YOUR HAIR IS GONE

JIM. (*crossing to DELLA*)
YOUR HAIR IS GONE
DELLA.
WHAT'S PAST IS PAST!
JIM.
YOUR HAIR IS GONE
DELLA.
IT GROWS SO FAST!

(*JIM sits in rocker and rocks in time to music.*)

JIM.	DELLA.
YOURHAIRISGONEYOUR	YESMYHAIRISGONEMY

HAIRISGONE	HAIRISGONE
YOURHAIRISGONEYOUR	MYHAIRISGONEMYHAIR
HAIRISGONE	ISGONEISGONE
YOURHAIRISGONEYOUR	YESMYHAIRISGONEMY
HAIRISGONE	HAIRISGONE
YOURHAIRISGONEYOUR	MYHAIRISGONEMYHAIR
HAIRISGONE	ISGONE

(*During the musical interlude JIM continues rocking in time. DELLA takes JIM's hat off and places it on the table. JIM holds his rock backwards when the music hesitates as if he is finally going to say something different, but then rocks forward again on:*)

JIM.
YOUR HAIR IS GONE
DELLA. (*slightly annoyed now*)
YOUR EYES ARE GOOD!
JIM.
YOUR HAIR IS GONE
DELLA.
I UNDERSTOOD!

(*JIM leaves rocker and walks upright on his knees towards DELLA who backs away.*)

JIM.	DELLA.
YOUR HAIR IS . . . GONE	I'M STILL THE SAME, JIM
YOUR HAIR IS GONE	I'M STILL THE SAME
YOUR HAIR IS . . . GONE	I'M STILL THE SAME, JIM
YOUR HAIR IS GONE	I'M STILL THE SAME

(*JIM stays walking upright on his knees for half of the next lyric, but then is standing and by the dressing table.*)

DELLA. (*aside*)	JIM. (*focused on her*)
WHEN I TELL HIM WHY I CUT IT	YOUR HAIR IS GONE
WILL HE LOVE ME LIKE BEFORE?	YOUR HAIR IS GONE
WILL HE WANT ME? WILL HE NEED ME?	YOUR HAIR IS GONE
WILL HE TAKE ME IN HIS ARMS AGAIN?	YOUR HAIR IS GONE

(*JIM takes hand mirror-frame only, no glass, from dressing table and holds it up to DELLA's face.*)

JIM.
YOUR HAIR IS GONE
DELLA.
PLEASE DON'T BE MAD!
JIM.
YOUR HAIR IS GONE
DELLA.
DOES IT LOOK BAD?

JIM.	DELLA.
YOURHAIRISGONEYOUR HAIRISGONE	YESMYHAIRISGONEMY HAIRISGONE
YOURHAIRISGONEYOUR HAIRISGONE	MYHAIRISGONEMYHAIR ISGONEISGONE
YOURHAIRISGONEYOUR HAIRISGONE	YESMYHAIRISGONEMY HAIRISGONE
YOURHAIRISGONEYOUR HAIRISGONE	MYHAIRISGONEMYHAIR ISGONE
YOUR HAIR IS GONE!	MY HAIR IS GONE!
YOUR HAIR IS GONE!	MY HAIR IS GONE!

(*The song ends, and JIM is staring at DELLA like a setter at the scent of a quail. It is an expression that she cannot read, and it terrifies her. It is not anger, or surprise, or disapproval, or horror—just a stare.*)

DELLA. Jim, darling. Don't look at me that way! I had my hair cut off and sold it because I couldn't have lived through Christmas without giving you a present. It'll grow out again—you won't mind will you? (*Pause. Jim just stares.*) I just had to do it. My hair grows awfully fast. Say "Merry Christmas," Jim, and let's be happy. You don't know what a nice—what a beautiful, nice gift I've got for you.

JIM. (*still dead-pan*) You've cut off your hair.

DELLA. Cut it off and sold it. Don't you like me just as well? I'm still me without my hair, aren't I? (*JIM looks under his hat on the table. Maybe he even looks in the stove.*)

JIM. You say your hair is gone.

DELLA. You needn't look for it. It's sold, I tell you—sold and gone, too. It's Christmas Eve, boy. Be good to me, for it went for you. Maybe the hairs of my head were numbered, but nobody could ever count my love for you. (*JIM wakes out of his trance and enfolds DELLA.*)

JIM. Don't make any mistake, Dell, about me. I don't think there's anything that could make me like my girl any less. Not a haircut, or a shampoo, or a shave . . . But if you'll unwrap that package—(*He points to dressing table where present is.*) you may see why you took me by surprise for a while there. (*DELLA runs to the dressing table, sits and opens the package excitedly . . . and there are The Combs! She lifts them in the air.*)

DELLA. Oh, Jim!

(*MUSIC CUE #11a—"Gift-Opening Music."*)

JIM. They're made of tortoise shell. They're the combs you had admired so many times in that little shop on Broadway, remember?

DELLA. Oh, yes, I remember. I worshipped these combs! But they were so expensive that I never dreamed that someday I could own them! Oh, thank you! They'll look so beautiful in—(*She suddenly remembers her hair is gone.*)—my hair!! Oh, Jim . . . (*DELLA makes a quick feminine change to tears and wails. JIM comforts her. DELLA recovers, and hugging the combs she looks up at JIM with dim eyes and a smile to say:*) My hair grows so fast, Jim! (*JIM laughs. Then DELLA leaps up like a little singed cat.*) Oh! Oh! I almost forgot! (*DELLA gets package from mantle.*) Look what my hair bought for you. (*She hands package to him . . . he hesitates.*) Go on! Open it! (*JIM opens the package and holds up the gold watch chain and fob.*) Isn't it a dandy, Jim! It's a gold chain and fob for your watch! I hunted all over town to find it. You'll have to look at the time a hundred times a day now! Give me your watch . . . I want to see how it looks on it.

(*The music stops. Instead of obeying, JIM turns and walks away a little. He then turns to DELLA and says:*)

JIM. Dell . . . let's put our Christmas presents away and keep them for a while . . . They're too nice to use just right now.

(*MUSIC CUE #12—"By the Way". JIM starts putting the presents away.*)

THE GIFT OF THE MAGI

Jim. (*singing*)
BY THE WAY
IN ORDER TO PURCHASE THESE COMBS FOR YOUR HAIR
I NEEDED SOME CASH
SO I STOPPED INTO A PAWN SHOP ON BROADWAY
AND GOT WITH LITTLE TROUBLE
A VERY GOOD PRICE . . . FOR MY WATCH . . .

    Della. (*spoken over music*) Your watch is gone?
    Jim. Dell . . . You are my only real treasure . . .

(*They slowly walk towards each other. MUSIC CUE #13— "End Scene 2".*)

Both. (*singing*)
ALL I REALLY NEED DELL/JIM
IS YOU CLOSE BY MY SIDE

IT DOESN'T MATTER, I'D STILL BE IN BLISS
IF YOU GAVE ME THE WORLD OR JUST GAVE ME A KISS
AND AS LONG AS I'M NEAR YOU MY HEART SHALL PROCLAIM
FOREVER AND EVER
FOREVER AND EVER . . . I'LL LOVE YOU THE SAME!
(*They end In an embrace.*)

(*MUSIC CUE #14— "Bows and Tomorrow is Christmas (reprise)." When they begin the reprise JIM and DELLA take out strings of popcorn and snowflakes made of newspaper and decorate the flat as they sing. Near the end of the reprise they produce a sprig of mistletoe which they hang from one of the gas lamps, and they end underneath it with a kiss.*)

Both. (*singing*)
TOMORROW IS CHRISTMAS, THE TIME TO BE MERRY
WITH WREATHES TIED WITH RIBBONS AS RED AS A BERRY
THE CANDLES AND HOLLY CHASE WORRIES AWAY
FOR TOMORROW IS CHRISTMAS DAY . . .

TOMORROW IS CHRISTMAS WHEN SPIRITS ARE
  LIGHTER
THE SPARKLE OF SNOW MAKES THE CITY SEEM
  BRIGHTER
AND EVERYTHING LOOKS LIKE A WINDOW DISPLAY
FOR TOMORROW IS CHRISTMAS DAY . . .

LOOK OUTSIDE AND A STAR ABOVE
WILL SHINE AS A GUIDE TO US ALL
JOY WILL COME WHEN WE GIVE OUR LOVE
NO MATTER HOW GREAT OR HOW SMALL

A SMILE IN THE MORNING, A CHILD IN A MANGER
A GIFT FROM THE HEART TO A FRIEND OR A
  STRANGER
THE WARMTH OF A WORLD GETTING READY TO SAY
THAT TOMORROW IS CHRISTMAS, CHRISTMAS DAY!!
(*spoken*) Merry Christmas!!!

(*MUSIC CUE #15 — "Exit Music."*)

THE END

THE GIFT OF THE MAGI

COSTUMES

JIM (humble clerk look)
Red union suit: — faded and patched
Red and white striped shirt
   period white stiff collar
   cufflinks
Sepia toned suit (worn looking)
   Cutaway coat
   Suspenders
   Vest with watch pocket
Bow tie
Bowler hat
Socks — heavy dark wool
Tattered gloves
Overcoat
Muffler
Ankle high brown shoes with hooks
Wire framed glasses (optional)

DELLA
Long wig
Short wig
Bloomers
Camisole
Corset
Petticoat
Period hose (black or brown cotton)
Shirtwaist blouse with high collar (ecru)
Floor length wool skirt
Period boots (with hooks)
Shawl

THE GIFT OF THE MAGI
PROPERTY LIST

Furniture/set pieces (all period and humble):
Windows (at least one practical) — frosted
Snow machines
Window shutters (practical)
Bed — Mission or iron frame
Worn carpet
Chest
Armoire
Rocking chair
Hearth seat
Dresser with mirror frame (*no* glass)
Fireplace
Low sink
Stove
Coal bucket
Andirons
Cupboard
Kitchen table — round
2 kitchen chairs
Dressing table with splashboard and mirror frame (*no* glass)
Chair at dressing table
Coat tree

Props (practical — all must be period and humble):
Water pitcher
Wash basin
Bed linens
Bed spread: patchwork
Coffee cups
Coffee pot with coffee
Spoons
Milk bottle with milk
Shaving brush
Shaving soap
Razor: straight
Powder puff and jar
Hair pins
Brush
Muffin tin
Muffins
Hand towel

Dish towel
Hand mirror (frame only — no glass)
Broom
Sugar bowl
Stack of unpaid bills
Jar or can for pennies
187 pennies
Handkerchief for pennies
Madame Sofronie advertisement card
Wooden crate (small)
Strings of popcorn and newspaper snowflakes
Sprig of mistletoe
Gold pocket watch with leather strap
Two wrapped packages for The Gifts
Combs for Della
Gold watch chain and fob for Jim

Props (set dressing):
Clothes and linens in chest and armoire
Lumps of coal in coal bucket
Cupboard items: dishes, pots, pans, utensils, glasses, jars, food basics (salt, pepper, flour, coffee, etc.)
Toiletries on dressing table (tooth powder, talc, pomade — not too much)
A *few* evergreen branches on mantle and dresser
Bible

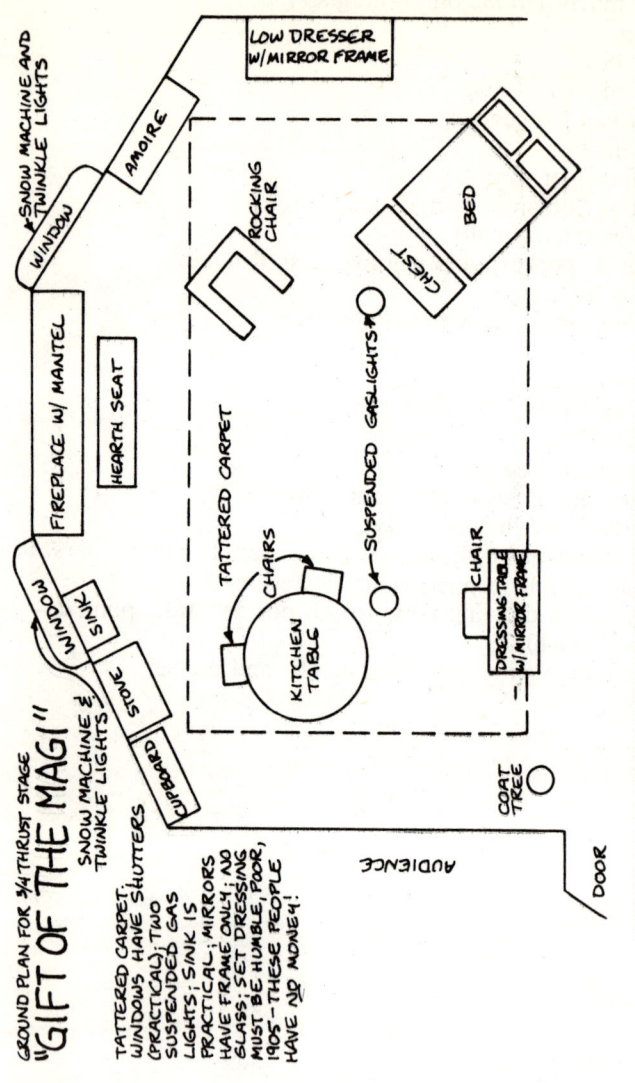